J j

Josef's Journal and the Letter J

Alphabet Friends

by Cynthia Klingel and Robert B. Noyed

**Published in the United States of America
by The Child's World®**
P.O. Box 326
Chanhassen, MN 55317-0326
800-599-READ
www.childsworld.com

The Child's World®: Mary Berendes, Publishing Director

Editorial Directions, Inc.: E. Russell Primm, Editorial
Director; Emily Dolbear, Line Editor; Ruth Martin,
Editorial Assistant; Linda S. Koutris, Photo Researcher
and Selector

Photographs ©: Corbis: Cover & 9, 17; Digital Vision/
Picture Quest: 10; Owaki-Kulla/Corbis: 13; Asian Art &
Archaeology, Inc./Corbis: 14; G. K. and Vikki Hart/
Brand X Pictures/Picture Quest: 18; Koopman/Corbis: 21.

Library of Congress Cataloging-in-Publication Data
Klingel, Cynthia Fitterer.
  Josef's journal and the letter J / by Cynthia Klingel
and Robert B. Noyed.
    p. cm. — (Alphabet readers)
Summary: A simple story about a boy named Josef and
the journal he keeps introduces the letter "j".
  ISBN 1-59296-100-2 (alk. paper)
  [1. Diaries—Fiction. 2. Alphabet.] I. Noyed, Robert B.
II. Title. III. Series.
  PZ7.K6798Jo 2003
  [E]—dc21
                                    2003006536

Note to parents and educators:
The first skill children acquire before becoming successful readers is individual letter recognition. The Alphabet Friends series has been created with the needs of young learners in mind. Each engaging book begins by showing the difference between the capital letter and the lowercase letter. In each of the books on the vowels and the consonants c and g, children are introduced to the different sounds that the letter can make. Finally, children see that the letters can be found at the beginning of a word, in the middle of a word, and in most cases, at the end of a word.

Following the introduction, children meet their Alphabet Friends. The friend in each story encounters many words that include the featured letter of that book. Each noun that begins with the title letter is highlighted in red with the initial letter of the word in bold. Above the word is a rebus drawing that establishes a strong picture cue.

At the end of each book, we have included three words lists. Can your young learners find all the words in each book with the title letter in them?

Let's learn about the letter **J.**

The letter **J** can look like this: **J.**

The letter **J** can also look like this: **j.**

The letter **j** can be at the

beginning of a word, like journal.

journal

The letter **j** can be in the

middle of a word, like flapjacks.

flap**j**acks

The English language doesn't have

any words that end in **j.**

My name is **J**osef. I have a **j**ournal. I

enjoy writing in my **j**ournal every day.

My friends are **J**ackson and **J**essie.

I write about them in my journal.

In my journal, I wrote about **Jackson's**

birthday. **Jackson** was born in **July.** I

gave him a joke book just for laughs.

In my journal, I wrote about Jackson's

trip to Japan. He bought me a jade

dog.

In my **j**ournal, I jotted down some notes

about **J**essie. She likes to eat **j**unk food.

Her favorite is **j**elly beans.

In my journal, I wrote about Jessie's

dance recital. Jessie danced a jazz

dance. She jumped across the stage.

My journal is just for me. I enjoy reading

the things I wrote about my friends

Jackson and Jessie.

Fun Facts

 Japan is an island country in the north Pacific Ocean. It lies off the eastern coast of the continent of Asia. Japan is made up of four big islands and lots of smaller ones. The Japanese call their country *Nihon* or *Nippon,* which means "origin of the sun." Japan's flag represents a red sun on a white background.

 Are you a fan of jelly beans? Lots of people are, especially around Easter time. In 1996, more than 13.5 billion jelly beans were enjoyed by Americans during the Easter holiday. If all those jelly beans were lined up end-to-end, they would circle Earth almost three times!

 July is the seventh month of the year. It was named after Julius Caesar, a Roman general and powerful ruler. The Romans originally called July *Quintilis,* which means "fifth," because it was the fifth month of their calendar year. Julius Caesar was born in Quintilis, so after he died, the month was named *Julius* in his honor.

To Read More

About the Letter J

Klingel, Cynthia. *Jump! The Sound of J.* Chanhassen, Minn.: The Child's World, 2000.

About Japan

Littlefield, Holly, and Helen Byers (illustrator). *Colors of Japan.* Minneapolis: Carolrhoda Books, 1992.

Pluckrose, Henry Arthur. *Japan.* Danbury, Conn.: Franklin Watts, 1998.

Schemenauer, Elma. *Japan.* Chanhassen, Minn.: The Child's World, 1998.

About Jelly Beans

Capucilli, Karen. *The Jelly Bean Fun Book.* New York: Little Simon, 2001.

Maw, Taylor. *The Incredible Jelly Bean Day.* Kansas City, Mo.: Landmark Editions, 1998.

About July

Brode, Robyn. *July.* Milwaukee, Wis.: Weekly Reader Early Learning Library, 2003.

Klingel, Cynthia, and Robert B. Noyed. *The Fourth of July.* Chanhassen, Minn.: The Child's World, 2003.

Watson, Wendy. *Hurray for the Fourth of July.* New York: Clarion Books, 1992.

Words with J

Words with J at the Beginning

Jackson

jade

Japan

jazz

jelly beans

Jessie

joke

Josef

jotted

journal

July

jumped

junk

just

Words with J in the Middle

enjoy

flapjacks

About the Authors

Cynthia Klingel has worked as a high school English teacher and an elementary teacher. She is currently the curriculum director for a Minnesota school district. Cynthia Klingel lives with her family in Mankato, Minnesota.

Robert B. Noyed started his career as a newspaper reporter. Since then, he has worked in communications and public relations for a Minnesota school district for more than fourteen years. Robert B. Noyed lives with his family in Brooklyn Center, Minnesota.